Jenny Ganther Braulick

August 31, 2007

Jenny Ganther Braulick

Kristy and the Secret of
Yesterday Farm

Kristy and the Secret of Yesterday Farm

Jenny Panther Braulick

Art by Mark Lipe and Veida Blick

The Editorial Annex

Oklahoma City/Edmond, Oklahoma

The Editorial Annex

Oklahoma City/Edmond, Oklahoma

Printed in China.

ISBN 0-9725012-3-1

To my husband, Todd, whose love lets me be who I am.

Looking around, Kristy saw she was the only one in a lacy dress. Everyone seemed to be in overalls and plaid shirts. She felt out of place…a little lost.

She had never been anywhere like this. The September air carried many smells— smoky coal and oil, buttery popcorn, hot caramel apples. Her ears picked up the happy melody of carousel music. She heard old farm engines running chug-a-chug, chug-a-chug. She was in Iowa at the Old Threshers Reunion.

Kristy moved closer to Gramps and clenched his big wrinkled hand. Gramps smiled at her. With the toe of his boot he kicked at the dusty walkway. "Let's play a game," he said.

"Oh good," said Kristy. "What kind?"

"A discovery game," said Gramps.

"Jumpin' Jellybeans," said Kristy. "A discovery about what?"

"About you," Gramps said.

"Me?"

"Yep. Who are you?" Gramps asked in a playful gruff voice.

"You know who I am," Kristy snapped back. "Kristin Marie McCormick."

"From where?" asked Gramps.

"Chicago," she said, lifting an eyebrow.

"Okay. You're Kristy from the big city," echoed Gramps. "That's part of it, but not all. Look at this."

"What is it?" asked Kristy.

"A plow," Gramps said. "One of the first farm tools. Used many years before you were born. Many things at this fair came from the early 1900s. Your Great-Great-Grandpa Joe worked this plow."

"How?" asked Kristy.

"A horse pulled it. Your Great Joe walked behind and guided it. The plow's sharp blade turned the soil, making it ready for planting crop seeds, like wheat. Can you see yourself alongside Great Joe?"

"No," gasped Kristy. "Me? Behind a plow?" She started to laugh out loud at the thought, but felt Gramp's blue eyes bearing down on her like a wise old owl. No doubt about it. He was up to something. "Why do you ask?" Her voice oozed with suspicion.

Gramps arched his bushy eyebrows.

"Oh—I get it!" Kristy blurted out. "Great Joe and the plow. They're clues to the game we're playing, aren't they?"

"Yep. Take a guess," Gramps said.

"Great Joe was a farmer, right?" Kristy guessed boldly.

"That's part of it, but not all," Gramps said, looking pleased with himself.

"What does a plow have to do with me?" Kristy wondered.

Gramps led Kristy to a big machine with a smoke stack. "It's a steam engine."

"How does it make steam?" she asked.

"Coal burns inside the engine and puts off heat. That heat turns water into steam. The steam makes the engine's wheels turn."

Gramp's wise eyes searched Kristy's face as if she should know something.

"Is this another clue in your strange game?" she asked.

Gramps chuckled. "Of course."

Kristy thought for a minute. "Great Joe used the steam engine to make his work easier," she guessed. "Is that it?"

"That's part of it, but not all," said Gramps.

"Jumpin' Jellybeans! This game is hard." Kristy followed Gramps to another machine. It had a long neck. "How odd."

"It's called a thresher," said Gramps. "Farmers put wheat stalks in the machine's round part, the feeder. The stalks are pounded 'til all the grain is removed. A lift, called an elevator, hauls the grain to a wagon or a bag. Leftover straw is blown out through the thresher's long neck."

"Look!" cried Kristy. "That big belt from a steam engine goes to the threshing machine and makes it run."

"Sure does. Can you see yourself carrying drinking water to the threshers, the men running the machine?"

"Not in my fancy dress," Kristy answered in a firm voice.

Gramps smiled. "Your Great-Great - Grandma Elizabeth did many times."

"Was she like me?" Kristy asked.

"Yep. Very much. Can you guess how?" Gramps asked.

13

Kristy shook her head. She had no idea how she was like Great Elizabeth.

Toot! Toot!

"Look! A train." Kristy pulled Gramps toward it.

"See that pointed grill on the front of the locomotive? That's a cowcatcher," Gramps said. "Long ago on the open prairie, cows sometimes got on the tracks. The train had to slow down and use its cowcatcher to nudge the cows out of the way."

"Did it hurt the cows?"

"No, they were gently pushed off the tracks," Gramps said. "Did you know your Great-Great-Uncle John was an engineer on the Midwest Railroad?"

"Wow," said Kristy. "Did he carry food from Great Joe's farm?"

"Sure did," replied Gramps. "Took corn, beans, cows to be sold in the city."

"Was it a big farm?" she asked. "Who's farm?" Gramps eyed her hard.

"Great Joe's—our farm," she said.

Gramps grinned, a twinkle in his eye. "You're getting warm. Can you guess?"

Kristy rolled her eyes and took a wild guess. "Our family farm was big?"

"That's part of it, but not all."

Kristy stomped her foot. "What is it I'm supposed to find out?"

Gramps pointed to a log house. "That's how your Great-Great-Grandma Elizabeth lived. She washed her family's clothes outside in large tubs. She made her own soap out of butter, oils, and lye. Her little girl, who looked a lot like you, hung the clothes on a line to dry. The potatoes, onions, and tomatoes they ate were grown in their garden. Her little boy had to weed the garden and keep it plowed and watered."

"That's a lot of work."

"Yep," answered Gramps. "They even sewed their own clothes and stitched quilts for their bed."

"I have chores to do," said Kristy. "But I sure don't work that hard."

"Back then," Gramps said, "there weren't so many big city girls like you. Back then, you might've lived on a farm."

"Huh? Me on a farm? That's silly!"

16

"Not as silly as you may think," Gramps hooted.

"Oh," Kristy said, seeing that Gramps meant business. "Me on a farm? Is that a clue to our game? Me on a farm?"

"That's part of it, but not all. What's that got to do with you today?"

Kristy was more confused than ever. She stepped inside the log house. A black stove with curved legs caught her eye.

"It's a wood-burning stove," Gramps explained. "It was used for both cooking and heating the house."

Kristy frowned. "That stove doesn't look like it could put out much heat. Wasn't Great Elizabeth cold in winter?"

Gramps put his arm around her. "Don't worry. She kept warm. She wore layers of clothing and wrapped up in blankets."

"What about summer? How did she keep cool in hot weather?" Kristy asked.

"She did hard chores just after the sun came up and at the close of day. It was cooler then. Summer was very important."

"Why?" asked Kristy.

"Summer was the time farmers tended crops, put up food, and chopped wood for the winter. This work had to be done in summer. In autumn they were too busy in the field, harvesting corn and beans."

Kristy thought about doing those kind of chores. "I couldn't live on a farm."

"Sure you could," said Gramps as they strolled toward the horse stables. "Can you see yourself taking care of horses?"

"Oh yes," Kristy said. "I love horses."

"Horses were one of the first sources of power. They pulled plows and wagons," Gramps explained.

"And people rode them," Kristy added. Gramps nodded. "Yep. Great Joe had lots of horses. Other animals were important, too. Cows, chickens, pigs."

"Jumpin' Jellybeans! I couldn't care for pigs," Kristy said, wrinkling her nose.

"Sure you could."

"Never. I'm a city girl, not a farm girl."

Gramps chuckled. "In some ways we're all from the farm. Especially you. Can you guess how?"

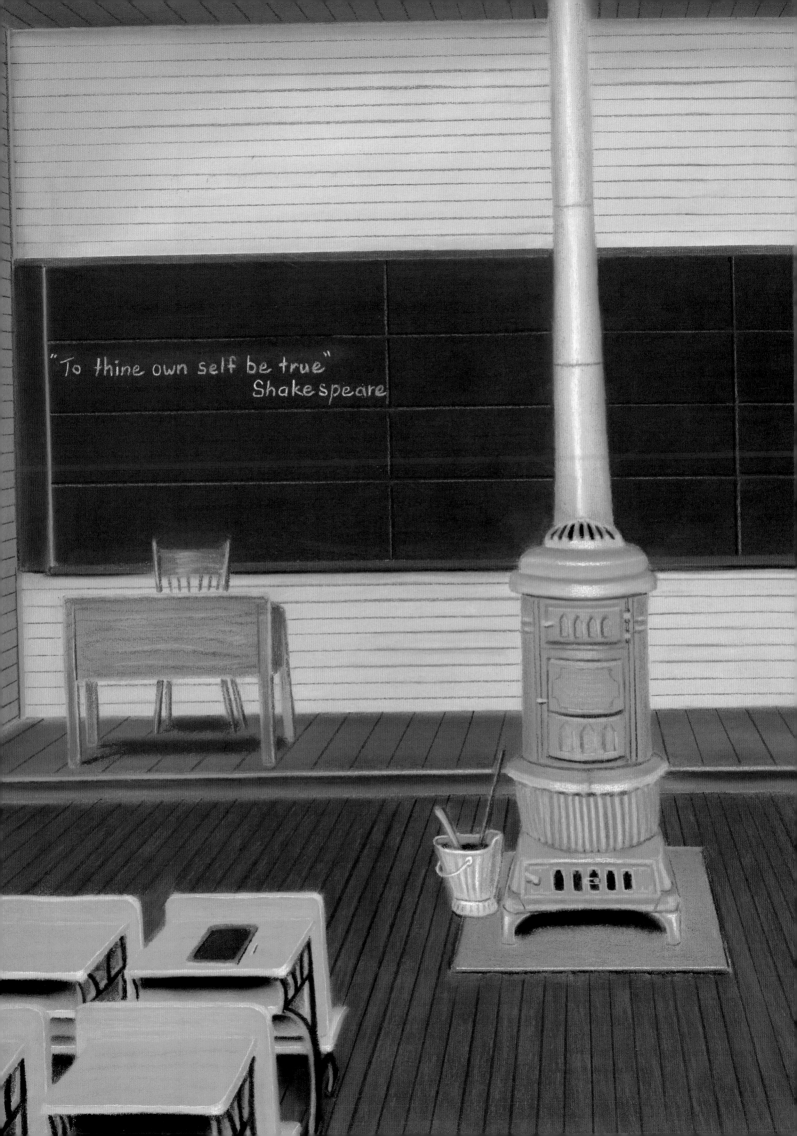

"This game is strange," Kristy complained. "It must have something to do with my great-great-grandparents."

"That's part of it, but not all."

Kristy huffed out loud. "What's the rest of it?"

Across the Old Threshers grounds stood The Old Time Town. It had a wood-front general store, post office, jail, and blacksmith shop. On Main Street was a schoolhouse. Kristy and Gramps went in.

Inside were little wooden desks with chalk slates for writing. "This is a one-room schoolhouse," Gramps said. "Children of all ages studied together in one small room like this."

"All grades together?" asked Kristy.

"All eight grades. Your Great-Great-Aunt Jen taught in a room like this. Farm kids got up at dawn, milked the cows, and hiked to school by 9 o'clock sharp."

"I bet their lessons were easier than this game of yours," Kristy said. "Your clues are so hard."

"Give up?" said Gramps, teasing her.

Kristy crossed her arms. How easy it would be to give up. But instead she heard herself declare: "Never! I'm not going to let you win—you wise old owl."

Gramps laughed. "So, take a guess."

"Okay. Long ago, my farm family attended class in a one-room schoolhouse."

"That's part of it, but not all."

"Jumpin' Jellybeans! Stop saying that," exclaimed Kristy.

Across the street was the general store. "Look at all these clothes," Kristy said.

"Try something on." Gramps held up an outfit. "How about this?"

Kristy eyed the overalls and checkered shirt. She paused, her finger on her chin, then nodded. "Okay, I'll put them on."

She buckled the overall straps and stepped out of the dressing room.

"What d'ya think?" Gramps asked.

Kristy shrugged, "Fine, I guess." She studied Gramp's weathered face, wondering what he was thinking.

"Look in the mirror," said Gramps. "What d'ya see?"

Kristy gazed at her reflection. "I see myself in farm clothes," she said.

"Look deeper," Gramps said.

Kristy stared hard into the mirror. Suddenly, she could see herself helping Great Joe plow the field, Great Elizabeth carry water to the threshers, Great John run the train, and Great Jen teach school.

"What d'ya see?" Gramps asked again.

Kristy blinked. "I see myself. I'm a farm girl. Not all of me, but part of me."

"That's it! You got it!" Gramps gave Kristy a big hug. She pulled away.

"Gramps," Kristy said in a worried voice, "what if I hadn't gotten it?"

"You'd be lost."

"Lost?"

"Yep. You're lost 'til you know the past, the part that makes you who you are. You can't grow up 'til you know who you are."

Kristy grinned. "Gramps, I just love your games!" She put her hand in his and they left the Old Threshers Reunion. Kristy proudly wore her farm clothes all the way home to the big city.

26

About the Old Threshers Reunion

Before there was gasoline, there was steam. Before electricity, there were hand-operated washing machines. Before combines, there were threshing machines.

Each year, at the close of summer, the Old Threshers Reunion takes visitors back to that time—the early 1900s when horses, fire, water, and old-fashioned elbow grease fueled the nation's agricultural industry.

The Old Threshers Reunion began more than half a century ago. It was the idea of a few agrarian history buffs in Mt. Pleasant, a Norman Rockwell style town in the southeast corner of Iowa.

Today, always the five days ending Labor Day, more than 80,000 visitors annually flock to the Reunion. It's the largest party of its kind celebrating the challenges farm families overcame and the accomplishments they made along the way.

At every turn, visitors discover story-telling artifacts and exhibits. Heritage museums highlight American farm implements, the role of water, how electricity changed the farm, and women's contributions to the land. Also to be explored is an old-time town complete with a general store and one-room schoolhouse.

New to the lore of this history-laden site is the tale of *Kristy and the Secret of Yesterday Farm*. Many real-life visitors at the Old Threshers Reunion are like Kristy. They glimpse the past and come away with a deeper awareness of their own reality.

For more about the Old Threshers Reunion, call 319-385-8937 or visit www.oldthreshers.com.

Acknowledgments

I am grateful for the generous cooperation and assistance from the following organizations and individuals: Old Threshers, Inc., Mt. Pleasant, Iowa; Christie Vilsack, First Lady of Iowa; M. Jean Greenlaw, Professor Emeritus, University of North Texas; Max Lucado, minister and best-selling author; and Richard M. Crum, my publisher, editor, and mentor.

The Editorial Annex
Oklahoma City/Edmond, Oklahoma

The Editorial Annex is a
communications consultancy and publishing house
founded in Washington, D.C., 1991.

Editor & Publisher
Richard M. Crum
www.theeditorialannex.com

Design
Felton Stroud
Stroud Design, Inc., Oklahoma City, OK
www.strouddesign.com

Author's Website
www.jumpinjellybeans.net

Typeset in 13 point Caxton Book with 26 point leading.
Title and accent text in Caxton Bold.

Printing and binding through InterPress Limited.
Four-color process inks on 106 lb. opaque text.
Dust jacket printed in four-color process inks on 106 lb. gloss enamel.
Smythe-sewn case binding with four-color laminated board.